You Are To Me

written and illustrated by

Rebecca Doughty

G.P. Putnam's Sons   New York

Published simultaneously in Canada. Manufactured in China by South China Printing Co. Ltd.
Jacket designed by Carolyn T. Fucile. Text set in Gill Sans.
The art was done in Flashe paint and ink on bristol board.
Library of Congress Cataloging-in-Publication Data
Doughty, Rebecca.   You are to me / written and illustrated by Rebecca Doughty.
p. cm.   Summary: A pig expresses how much he thinks of and cares for his rabbit friend.
[1. Friendship—Fiction. 2. Pigs—Fiction. 3. Rabbits—Fiction. 4. Stories in rhyme.] I. Title.
PZ8.3.D743Yo 2004   [E]—dc21   2003008522

ISBN 0-399-24176-0
1   3   5   7   9   10   8   6   4   2
First Impression

for my wonderful friends
who are to me...
and especially
in memory of David

-RD

I believe
you are to me...

the very best

the best can be.

You're
peanut butter
chocolate
chip,

you're double dip and triple flip,

you're roller skate,

you're sun and moon,

you're bicycle,

you're May and June,

you're dandelion

and
daffodil,

you're slippery sled

and snowy hill,

you're butterfly

and pussy willow,

you're
furry ted

and feather pillow,

you're orange juice

and clementine,

you're
pony ride,

you're
bunny hug,

you're water slide,

You're ultrabest, the superfest,

you're
marvelest,

you're
bluebird nest.

You're you-est you,
you're yes-sir-ee,

you're ABSO-BESTO-lu-tel-y!

I'm telling you

so you will see...

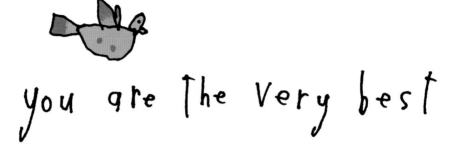

you are the very best

to me.

WITHDRAWN